Henry Walter   Worth

Ground Tumbling

Henry Walter   Worth

Ground Tumbling

ISBN/EAN: 9783337365332

Printed in Europe, USA, Canada, Australia, Japan

Cover: Foto ©Andreas Hilbeck / pixelio.de

More available books at **www.hansebooks.com**

A. G. Spalding & Bros.
MAINTAIN THEIR OWN HOUSES FOR DISTRIBUTING
THE
Spalding
COMPLETE LINE OF
Athletic Goods
IN THE FOLLOWING CITIES

NEW YORK
  Downtown-
    124–128 Nassau St.
  Uptown-
    29–33 West 42d St.
NEWARK, N. J.
    845 Broad Street

BOSTON, MASS.
141 Federal Street

CHICAGO
147–149 Wabash Ave.
ST. LOUIS, MO.
415 North Seventh St.
KANSAS CITY, MO.
1120 Grand Ave.
DENVER, COL.
1616 Arapahoe St.

SAN FRANCISCO
156–158 Geary St.
SEATTLE, WASH.
711 Second Ave.
LOS ANGELES, CAL.
435 South Spring St.

BUFFALO, N. Y.
611 Main Street
SYRACUSE, N. Y.
University Block
PITTSBURG, PA.
439 Wood Street

CINCINNATI, O.
119 East Fifth St.
CLEVELAND, O.
741 Euclid Ave.
COLUMBUS, O.
191 South High St.

MILWAUKEE, WIS.
379 East Water St.
MINNEAPOLIS, MINN.
44 Seventh St., South
ST. PAUL, MINN.
386 Minnesota St.

PHILADELPHIA, PA.
1210 Chestnut Street
BALTIMORE, MD.
208 East Baltimore St.

4

WASHINGTON, D. C.
709 14th St., N.W.

DETROIT, MICH.
254 Woodward Ave.
LOUISVILLE, KY.
328 West Jefferson St.
INDIANAPOLIS, IND.
211 Massachusetts Ave.

ATLANTA, GA.
74 N. Broad Street
NEW ORLEANS, LA.
140 Carondelet St.
DALLAS, TEX.
355 Commerce St.

LONDON, ENG.
Three Stores
317–318,
High Holborn, W. C.

78, Cheapside
West End Branch
29, Haymarket, S.W.

BIRMINGHAM, ENG.
57, New Street
MANCHESTER, ENG.
4, Oxford St. and
1, Lower Moseley St.
EDINBURGH, SCOT.
3 South Charlotte St.
(Cor. Princes St.)

MONTREAL, P. Q.
443 St. James St.
TORONTO, ONT.
189 Yonge St.

SYDNEY, AUSTRALIA
228 Clarence St.

Communications directed to A.

5

G. SPALDING & BROS., at any
of the above addresses, will
receive prompt attention.

THE SPALDING
TRADE MARK IS
REGISTERED IN
THE UNITED
STATES PATENT
OFFICE, ALSO IN
27 FOREIGN
COUNTRIES.
INFRINGERS ARE
WARNED.

THE SPALDING TRADE-MARK IS THE
FOUNDATION OF THE SPALDING
BUSINESS

Spalding's Athletic Library

A. G. SPALDING

Anticipating the present tendency of the American people toward a healthful method of living and enjoyment, Spalding's Athletic Library was established in 1892 for the purpose of encouraging athletics in every form, not only by publishing the official rules and records pertaining to the various pastimes, but also by instructing, until to-day Spalding's Athletic Library is unique in its own particular field and has been conceded the greatest educational series on athletic and physical training subjects that has ever been compiled.

The publication of a distinct series of books devoted to athletic sports and pastimes and designed to occupy the premier place in America in its class was an early idea of Mr. A. G. Spalding, who was one of the first in America to publish a handbook devoted to athletic sports, Spalding's Official Base Ball Guide being the initial number, which was followed at intervals with other handbooks on the sports prominent in the '70s.

Spalding's Athletic Library has had the advice and counsel of Mr. A. G. Spalding in all of its undertakings, and particularly in all books devoted to the national game. This applies especially to Spalding's Official Base Ball Guide and Spalding's Official Base Ball Record, both of which receive the personal attention of Mr. A. G. Spalding, owing to his early connection with the game as the leading pitcher of the champion Boston and Chicago teams of 1872–76. His interest does not stop, however, with matters pertaining to base ball; there is not a sport that Mr. Spalding does not make it his business to become familiar with, and that the Library will always maintain its premier place, with Mr. Spalding's able counsel at hand, goes without saying.

The entire series since the issue of the first number has been under the direct personal supervision of Mr. James E. Sullivan, President of the American Sports Publishing Company, and the total series of consecutive numbers reach an aggregate of considerably over three hundred, included in which are many "annuals," that really constitute the history of their particular sport in America year by year, back copies of which are even now eagerly sought for, constituting as they do the really first authentic records of events and official rules that have ever been consecutively compiled.

When Spalding's Athletic Library was founded, seventeen years ago, track and field athletics were practically unknown outside the larger colleges and a few athletic clubs in the leading cities, which gave occasional meets, when an entry list of 250 competitors was a subject of comment; golf was known only by a comparatively few persons; lawn tennis had some vogue and base ball was practically the only established field sport, and that in a professional way; basket ball had just been invented; athletics for the schoolboy—and schoolgirl—were almost unknown, and an advocate of class contests in athletics in the schools could not get a hearing. To-day we find the greatest body of athletes in the world is the Public Schools Athletic League of Greater New York, which has had an entry list at its annual games of over two thousand, and in whose "elementary series" in base ball last year 106 schools competed for the trophy emblematic of the championship.

While Spalding's Athletic Library cannot claim that the rapid growth of athletics in this country is due to it solely, the fact cannot be denied that the books have had a great deal to do with its encouragement, by printing the official rules and instructions for playing the various games at a nominal price, within the reach of everyone, with the sole object that its series might be complete and the one place where a person could look with absolute certainty for the particular book in which he might be interested.

In selecting the editors and writers for the various books, the leading authority in his particular line has been obtained, with the result that no collection of books on athletic subjects can compare with Spalding's Athletic Library for the prominence of the various authors and their ability to present their subjects in a thorough and practical manner.

A short sketch of a few of those who have edited some of the leading numbers of Spalding's Athletic Library is given herewith:

JAMES E. SULLIVAN

President American Sports Publishing Company; entered the publishing house of Frank Leslie in 1878, and has been connected continuously with the publishing business since then and also as athletic editor of various New York papers; was a competing athlete; one of the organizers of the Amateur Athletic Union of the United States; has been actively on its board of governors since its organization until the present time, and President for two successive terms; has attended every championship meeting in America since 1879 and has officiated in some capacity in connection with American amateur championship track and field games for nearly twenty-five years; assistant American director Olympic Games, Paris, 1900; director Pan-American Exposition athletic department, 1901; chief department physical culture Louisiana Purchase Exposition, St. Louis, 1904; secretary American Committee Olympic Games, at Athens, 1906; honorary director of Athletics at Jamestown Exposition, 1907; secretary American Committee Olympic Games, at London, 1908; member of the Pastime A. C., New York; honorary member Missouri A. C., St. Louis; honorary member Olympic A. C., San Francisco; ex-president Pastime A. C., New Jersey A. C., Knickerbocker A. C.; president Metropolitan Association of the A. A. U. for fifteen years; president Outdoor Recreation League; with Dr. Luther H. Gulick organized the Public Schools Athletic League of New York, and is now chairman of its games committee and member executive committee; was a pioneer in playground work and one of the organizers of the Outdoor Recreation League of New York; appointed by President Roosevelt as special commissioner to the Olympic Games at Athens, 1906, and decorated by King George I. of the Hellenes (Greece) for his services in connection with the Olympic Games; appointed special commissioner by President Roosevelt to the Olympic Games at London, 1908; appointed by Mayor McClellan, 1908, as member of the Board of Education of Greater New York.

WALTER CAMP

For quarter of a century Mr. Walter Camp of Yale has occupied a leading position in college athletics. It is immaterial what organization is suggested for college athletics, or for the betterment of conditions, insofar as college athletics is concerned, Mr. Camp has always played an important part in its conferences, and the great interest in and high plane of college sport to-day, are undoubtedly due more to Mr. Camp than to any other individual. Mr. Camp has probably written more on college athletics than any other writer and the leading papers and magazines of America are always anxious to secure his expert opinion on foot ball, track and field athletics, base ball and rowing. Mr. Camp has grown up with Yale athletics and is a part of Yale's remarkable athletic system. While he has been designated as the "Father of Foot Ball," it is a well-known fact that during his college career Mr. Camp was regarded as one of the best players that ever represented Yale on the base ball field, so when we hear of Walter Camp as a foot ball expert we must also remember his remarkable knowledge of the game of base ball, of which he is a great admirer. Mr. Camp has edited Spalding's Official Foot Ball Guide since it was first published, and also the Spalding Athletic Library book on How to Play Foot Ball. There is certainly no man in American college life better qualified to write for Spalding's Athletic Library than Mr. Camp.

DR. LUTHER HALSEY GULICK

The leading exponent of physical training in America; one who has worked hard to impress the value of physical training in the schools; when physical training was combined with education at the St. Louis Exposition in 1904 Dr. Gulick played an important part in that congress; he received several awards for his good work and had many honors conferred upon him; he is the author of a great many books on the subject; it was Dr. Gulick, who, acting on the suggestion of James E. Sullivan, organized the Public Schools Athletic League of Greater New York, and was its first Secretary; Dr. Gulick was also for several years Director of Physical Training in the public schools of Greater New York, resigning the position to assume the Presidency of the Playground Association of America. Dr. Gulick is an authority on all subjects pertaining to physical training and the study of the child.

JOHN B. FOSTER

Successor to the late Henry Chadwick ("Father of Base Ball") as editor of Spalding's Official Base Ball Guide; sporting editor of the New York Evening Telegram; has been in the newspaper business for many years and is recognized throughout America as a leading writer on the national game; a staunch supporter of organized base ball, his pen has always been used for the betterment of the game.

TIM MURNANE

Base Ball editor of the Boston Globe and President of the New England League of Base Ball Clubs; one of the best known base ball men of the country; known from coast to coast; is a keen follower of the game and prominent in all its councils; nearly half a century ago was one of America's foremost players; knows the game thoroughly and writes from the point of view both of player and an official.

HARRY PHILIP BURCHELL

Sporting editor of the New York Times; graduate of the University of Pennsylvania; editor of Spalding's Official Lawn Tennis Annual; is an authority on the game;

follows the movements of the players minutely and understands not only tennis but all other subjects that can be classed as athletics; no one is better qualified to edit this book than Mr. Burchell.

GEORGE T. HEPBRON

Former Young Men's Christian Association director; for many years an official of the Athletic League of Young Men's Christian Associations of North America; was connected with Dr. Luther H. Gulick in Young Men's Christian Association work for over twelve years; became identified with basket ball when it was in its infancy and has followed it since, being recognized as the leading exponent of the official rules; succeeded Dr. Gulick as editor of the Official Basket Ball Guide and also editor of the Spalding Athletic Library book on How to Play Basket Ball.

JAMES S. MITCHEL

Former champion weight thrower; holder of numerous records, and is the winner of more championships than any other individual in the history of sport; Mr. Mitchel is a close student of athletics and well qualified to write upon any topic connected with athletic sport; has been for years on the staff of the New York Sun.

MICHAEL C. MURPHY

The world's most famous athletic trainer; the champion athletes that he has developed for track and field sports, foot ball and base ball fields, would run into thousands; he became famous when at Yale University and has been particularly successful in developing what might be termed championship teams; his rare good judgment has placed him in an enviable position in the athletic world; now with the University of Pennsylvania; during his career has trained only at two colleges and one athletic club, Yale and the University of Pennsylvania, and Detroit Athletic Club; his most recent triumph was that of training the famous American team of athletes that swept the field at the Olympic Games of 1908 at London.

DR. C. WARD CRAMPTON

Succeeded Dr. Gulick as director of physical training in the schools of Greater New York: as secretary of the Public Schools Athletic League is at the head of the most remarkable organization of its kind in the world; is a practical athlete and gymnast himself, and has been for years connected with the physical training system in the schools of Greater New York, having had charge of the High School of Commerce.

DR. GEORGE J. FISHER

Has been connected with Y. M. C. A. work for many years as physical director at Cincinnati and Brooklyn, where he made such a high reputation as organizer that he was chosen to succeed Dr. Luther H. Gulick as Secretary of the Athletic League of Y. M. C. A.'s of North America, when the latter resigned to take charge of the physical training in the Public Schools of Greater New York.

DR. GEORGE ORTON

On athletics, college athletics, particularly track
and field, foot ball, soccer foot ball, and training of the
youth, it would be hard to find one better qualified than Dr.
Orton; has had the necessary athletic experience and the
ability to impart that experience intelligently to the youth of
the land; for years was the American, British and Canadian
champion runner.

FREDERICK R. TOOMBS

A well-known authority on skating, rowing,
boxing, racquets, and other athletic sports; was sporting
editor of American Press Association, New York; dramatic
editor; is a lawyer and has served several terms as a member
of Assembly of the Legislature of the State of New York; has
written several novels and historical works.

R. L. WELCH

A resident of Chicago; the popularity of indoor
base ball is chiefly due to his efforts; a player himself of no
mean ability; a first-class organizer; he has followed the
game of indoor base ball from its inception.

DR. HENRY S. ANDERSON

Has been connected with Yale University for
years and is a recognized authority on gymnastics; is
admitted to be one of the leading authorities in America on
gymnastic subjects; is the author of many books on physical
training.

CHARLES M. DANIELS

Just the man to write an authoritative book on swimming; the fastest swimmer the world has ever known; member New York Athletic Club swimming team and an Olympic champion at Athens in 1906 and London, 1908. In his book on Swimming, Champion Daniels describes just the methods one must use to become an expert swimmer.

GUSTAVE BOJUS

Mr. Bojus is most thoroughly qualified to write intelligently on all subjects pertaining to gymnastics and athletics; in his day one of America's most famous amateur athletes; has competed successfully in gymnastics and many other sports for the New York Turn Verein; for twenty years he has been prominent in teaching gymnastics and athletics; was responsible for the famous gymnastic championship teams of Columbia University; now with the Jersey City high schools.

CHARLES JACOBUS

Admitted to be the "Father of Roque;" one of America's most expert players, winning the Olympic Championship at St. Louis in 1904; an ardent supporter of the game and follows it minutely, and much of the success of roque is due to his untiring efforts; certainly there is no one better qualified to write on this subject than Mr. Jacobus.

DR. E. B. WARMAN

Well known as a physical training expert; was probably one of the first to enter the field and is the author of many books on the subject; lectures extensively each year all over the country.

W. J. CROMIE

Now with the University of Pennsylvania; was formerly a Y. M. C. A. physical director; a keen student of all gymnastic matters; the author of many books on subjects pertaining to physical training.

G. M. MARTIN

By profession a physical director of the Young Men's Christian Association; a close student of all things gymnastic, and games for the classes in the gymnasium or clubs.

PROF. SENAC

A leader in the fencing world; has maintained a fencing school in New York for years and developed a great many champions; understands the science of fencing thoroughly and the benefits to be derived therefrom.

SPALDING ATHLETIC LIBRARY
Giving the Titles of all Spalding Athletic Library Books now in print, grouped for ready reference

SPALDING OFFICIAL ANNUALS

No. 1   Spalding's Official Base Ball Guide

No. 1A   Spalding's Official Base Ball Record
No. 2   Spalding's Official Foot Ball Guide
No. 2A   Spalding's Official Soccer Foot Ball Guide
No. 3   Spalding's Official Cricket Guide
No. 4   Spalding's Official Lawn Tennis Annual
No. 5   Spalding's Official Golf Guide
No. 6   Spalding's Official Ice Hockey Guide
No. 7   Spalding's Official Basket Ball Guide
No. 7A   Spalding's Official Women's Basket Ball Guide
No. 8   Spalding's Official Lacrosse Guide
No. 9   Spalding's Official Indoor Base Ball Guide
No. 10   Spalding's Official Roller Polo Guide
No. 12   Spalding's Official Athletic Almanac
No. 12A   Spalding's Official Athletic Rules

Group
I.   Base Ball

No. 1   *Spalding's Official Base Ball Guide*
No. 1A   Official Base Ball Record.
No. 202   How to Play Base Ball.
No. 223   How to Bat.
No. 232   How to Run Bases.
No. 230   How to Pitch.
No. 229   How to Catch.
No. 225   How to Play First Base.
No. 226   How to Play Second Base.
No. 227   How to Play Third Base.
No. 228   How to Play Shortstop.
No. 224   How to Play the Outfield.

No. 231   { How to Organize a Base Ball League.

                { How to Organize a Base Ball Club.

                { How to Manage a Base Ball Club.

                { How to Train a Base Ball Team.

                { How to Captain a Base Ball Team.

                { How to Umpire a Game.

                { Technical Base Ball Terms.

No. 219   Ready Reckoner of Base Ball Percentages.

BASE BALL AUXILIARIES

No. 336   Minor League Base Ball Guide.

No. 338   Official Book National League of Prof. Base Ball Clubs.

No. 340   Official Handbook National Playground Ball Assn.

Group II.   **Foot Ball**

No. 2   *Spalding's Official Foot Ball Guide.*

No. 334   Code of the Foot Ball Rules.

No. 324   How to Play Foot Ball.

No. 2A   *Spalding's Official Soccer Foot Ball Guide.*

No. 286   How to Play Soccer.

No. 335   English Rugby.

FOOT BALL AUXILIARY

No. 332   Spalding's Official Canadian Foot Ball Guide.

Group   **Cricket**
III.

No.   3   *Spalding's Official Cricket Guide.*
No. 277   Cricket; and How to Play It.

Group   **Lawn Tennis**
IV.

No.   4   *Spalding's Official Lawn Tennis Annual.*
No. 157   How to Play Lawn Tennis.
No. 279   Strokes and Science of Lawn Tennis.

Group   **Golf**
V.

No.   5   *Spalding's Official Golf Guide.*
No. 276   How to Play Golf.

Group   **Hockey**
VI.

No.   6   *Spalding's Official Ice Hockey Guide.*

No. 304   How to Play Ice Hockey.

No. 154   Field Hockey.

No. 188   {Lawn Hockey.
          {Parlor Hockey.
          {Garden Hockey.

No. 180   Ring Hockey.

HOCKEY AUXILIARY

No. 256   Official Handbook Ontario Hockey Association.

**Group
VII.**
                                    Basket Ball

No.   7   *Spalding's Official Basket Ball Guide.*

No.
7A   *Spalding's Official Women's Basket Ball Guide.*

No. 193   How to Play Basket Ball.

BASKET BALL AUXILIARY

No. 323   Official Collegiate Basket Ball Handbook.

**Group
VIII.**
                                    Lacrosse

Group XII.   Athletics

ATHLETIC AUXILIARIES

No. 339   Intercollegiate Official Handbook.

No. 302   Y. M. C. A. Official Handbook.

No. 313   Public Schools Athletic League Official
           Handbook.

No. 314   Public Schools Athletic League Official
           Handbook—Girls' Branch.

No. 308   Official Handbook New York Interscholastic
           Athletic Association.

Group   **Athletic Accomplishments**
XIII.

No. 177   How to Swim.

No. 296   Speed Swimming.

No. 128   How to Row.

No. 209   How to Become a Skater.

No. 178   How to Train for Bicycling.

No. 23   Canoeing.

No. 282   Roller Skating Guide.

Group   **Manly Sports**
XIV.

No. 18   Fencing. (By Breck.)

No. 162   Boxing.

No. 165   Fencing. (By Senac.)

Group XV.   **Gymnastics**

GYMNASTIC AUXILIARY

No. 333   Official Handbook I. C. A. A. Gymnasts of
          America.

Group   **Physical Culture**
XVI.

No. 161   Ten Minutes' Exercise for Busy Men.

No. 208   Physical Education and Hygiene.

No. 149   Scientific Physical Training and Care of the
          Body.

No. 142   Physical Training Simplified.

No. 185   Hints on Health.

No. 213   285 Health Answers.

No. 238   Muscle Building.

No. 234   School Tactics and Maze Running.

No. 261   Tensing Exercises.

No. 285   Health by Muscular Gymnastics.

No. 288   Indigestion Treated by Gymnastics.

No. 290   Get Well; Keep Well.

No. 325   Twenty-Minute Exercises.

No. 330   Physical Training for the School and Class
          Room.

ANY OF THE ABOVE BOOKS MAILED POSTPAID
UPON RECEIPT OF 10 CENTS

No. 1—Spalding's Official Base Ball Guide.

The leading Base Ball annual of the country, and the official authority of the game. Contains the official playing rules, with an explanatory index of the rules compiled by Mr. A. G. Spalding; pictures of all the teams in the National, American and minor leagues; reviews of the season; college Base Ball, and a great deal of interesting information. Price 10 cents.

No. 1A—Spalding's Official Base Ball Record.

Something new in Base Ball. Contains records of all kinds from the beginning of the National League and official averages of all professional organizations for past season. Illustrated with pictures of leading teams and players. Price 10 cents.

No. 202—How to Play Base Ball.

Edited by Tim Murnane. New and revised edition. Illustrated with pictures showing how all the various curves and drops are thrown and portraits of leading players. Price 10 cents.

No. 223—How to Bat.

There is no better way of becoming a proficient batter than by reading this book and practising the directions. Numerous illustrations. Price 10 cents.

No. 232—How to Run the Bases.

This book gives clear and concise directions for excelling as a base runner; tells when to run and when not to do so;

how and when to slide; team work on the bases; in fact, every point of the game is thoroughly explained. Illustrated. Price 10 cents.

No. 230—How to Pitch.

A new, up-to-date book. Its contents are the practical teaching of men who have reached the top as pitchers, and who know how to impart a knowledge of their art. All the big leagues' pitchers are shown. Price 10 cents.

No. 229—How to Catch.

Every boy who has hopes of being a clever catcher should read how well-known players cover their position. Pictures of all the noted catchers in the big leagues. Price 10 cents.

No. 225—How to Play First Base.

Illustrated with pictures of all the prominent first basemen. Price 10 cents.

No. 226—How to Play Second Base.

The ideas of the best second basemen have been incorporated in this book for the especial benefit of boys who want to know the fine points of play at this point of the diamond. Price 10 cents.

No. 227—How to Play Third Base.

Third base is, in some respects, the most important of the infield. All the points explained. Price 10 cents.

No. 228—How to Play Shortstop.

Shortstop is one of the hardest positions on the infield to fill, and quick thought and quick action are necessary for a player who expects to make good as a shortstop. Illus. Price 10 cents.

No. 224—How to Play the Outfield.

An invaluable guide for the outfielder. Price 10 cents.

No. 231—How to Coach; How to Captain a Team; How to Manage a Team; How to Umpire; How to Organize a League; Technical Terms of Base Ball.

A useful guide. Price 10 cents.

No. 219—Ready Reckoner of Base Ball Percentages.

To supply a demand for a book which would show the percentage of clubs without recourse to the arduous work of figuring, the publishers had these tables compiled by an expert. Price 10 cents.

BASE BALL AUXILIARIES.

No. 336—Minor League Base Ball Guide.

The minors' own guide. Edited by President T. H. Murnane, of the New England League. Price 10 cents.

No. 338—Official Handbook of the National League of Professional Base Ball Clubs.

Contains the Constitution, By-Laws, Official Rules, Averages, and schedule of the National League for the current year, together with list of club officers and reports of the annual meetings of the League. Price 10 cents.

No. 340—Official Handbook National Playground Ball Association.

This game is specially adapted for playgrounds, parks, etc., and is spreading rapidly. The book contains a description of the game, rules and list of officers. Price 10 cents.

No. 2—Spalding's Official Foot Ball Guide.

Edited by Walter Camp. Contains the new rules, with diagram of field; All-America teams as selected by the leading authorities; reviews of the game from various sections of the country; scores; pictures. Price 10 cents.

No. 334—Code of the Foot Ball Rules.

This book is meant for the use of officials, to help them to refresh their memories before a game and to afford them a quick means of ascertaining a point during a game. It also gives a ready means of finding a rule in the Official Rule Book, and is of great help to a player in studying the Rules. Compiled by C. W. Short, Harvard, 1908. Price 10 cents.

No. 324—How to Play Foot Ball.

Edited by Walter Camp, of Yale. Everything that a beginner wants to know and many points that an expert will be glad to learn. Snapshots of leading teams and players in action, with comments by Walter Camp. Price 10 cents.

No. 2A—Spalding's Official Association Soccer Foot Ball Guide.

A complete and up-to-date guide to the "Soccer" game in the United States, containing instructions for playing the game, official rules, and interesting news from all parts of the country. Illustrated. Price 10 cents.

No. 286—How to Play Soccer.

How each position should be played, written by the best player in England in his respective position, and illustrated with full-page photographs of players in action. Price 10 cents.

FOOT BALL AUXILIARIES.

No. 332—Spalding's Official Canadian Foot Ball Guide.

The official book of the game in Canada. Price 10 cents.

No. 335—Spalding's Official Rugby Foot Ball Guide.

Contains the official rules under which the game is played in England and by the California schools and colleges. Also instructions for playing the various positions on a team. Illustrated with action pictures of leading teams and players. Price 10 cents.

Group III.   Cricket

No. 3—Spalding's Official Cricket Guide.

The most complete year book of the game that has
ever been published in America. Reports of special
matches, official rules and pictures of all the leading teams.
Price 10 cents.

No. 277—Cricket; and How to Play it.

By Prince Ranjitsinhji. The game described concisely and
illustrated with full-page pictures posed especially for this
book. Price 10 cents.

No. 4—Spalding's Official Lawn Tennis Annual.

Contents include reports of all important tournaments; official ranking from 1885 to date; laws of lawn tennis; instructions for handicapping; decisions on doubtful points; management of tournaments; directory of clubs; laying out and keeping a court. Illustrated. Price 10 cents.

No. 157—How to Play Lawn Tennis.

A complete description of lawn tennis; a lesson for beginners and directions telling how to make the most important strokes. Illustrated. Price 10 cents.

No. 279—Strokes and Science of Lawn Tennis.

By P. A. Vaile, a leading authority on the game in Great Britain. Every stroke in the game is accurately illustrated and analyzed by the author. Price 10 cents.

No. 5—Spalding's Official Golf Guide.

Contains records of all important tournaments, articles on the game in various sections of the country, pictures of prominent players, official playing rules and general items of interest. Price 10 cents.

No. 276—How to Play Golf.

By James Braid and Harry Vardon, the world's two greatest players tell how they play the game, with numerous full-page pictures of them taken on the links. Price 10 cents.

No. 6—Spalding's Official Ice Hockey Guide.

The official year book of the game. Contains the official rules, pictures of leading teams and players, records, review of the season, reports from different sections of the United States and Canada. Price 10 cents.

No. 304—How to Play Ice Hockey.

Contains a description of the duties of each player. Illustrated. Price 10 cents.

No. 154—Field Hockey.

Prominent in the sports at Vassar, Smith, Wellesley, Bryn Mawr and other leading colleges. Price 10 cents.

No. 188—Lawn Hockey, Parlor Hockey, Garden Hockey.

Containing the rules for each game. Illustrated. Price 10 cents.

No. 180—Ring Hockey.

A new game for the gymnasium. Exciting as basket ball. Price 10 cents.

HOCKEY AUXILIARY.

No. 256—Official Handbook of the Ontario Hockey Association.

Contains the official rules of the Association, constitution, rules of competition, list of officers, and pictures of leading players. Price 10 cents.

No. 7—Spalding's Official Basket Ball Guide.

Edited by George T. Hepbron. Contains the revised official rules, decisions on disputed points, records of prominent teams, reports on the game from various parts of the country. Illustrated. Price 10 cents.

No. 7A—Spalding's Official Women's Basket Ball Guide.

Edited by Miss Senda Berenson, of Smith College. Contains the official playing rules and special articles on the game by prominent authorities. Illustrated. Price 10 cents.

No. 193—How to Play Basket Ball.

By G. T. Hepbron, editor of the Official Basket Ball Guide. Illustrated with scenes of action. Price 10 cents.

BASKET BALL AUXILIARY.

No. 323—Collegiate Basket Ball Handbook.

The official publication of the Collegiate Basket Ball Association. Contains the official rules, records, All-America selections, reviews, and pictures. Edited by H. A. Fisher, of Columbia. Price 10 cents.

Group VIII.   Lacrosse

No. 8—Spalding's Official Lacrosse Guide.

Contains the constitution, by-laws, playing rules, list of officers and records of the U. S. Inter-Collegiate Lacrosse League. Price 10 cents.

No. 201—How to Play Lacrosse.

Every position is thoroughly explained in a most simple and concise manner, rendering it the best manual of the game ever published. Illustrated with numerous snapshots of important plays. Price 10 cents.

Group IX.   Indoor Base Ball

No. 9—Spalding's Official Indoor Base Ball Guide.
America's national game is now vying with other indoor games as a winter pastime. This book contains the playing rules, pictures of leading teams, and interesting articles on the game by leading authorities on the subject. Price 10 cents.

Group X.

No. 10—Spalding's Official Roller Polo Guide.

Edited by J. C. Morse. A full description of the game; official rules; records; pictures of prominent players. Price 10 cents.

No. 129—Water Polo.

The contents of this book treat of every detail, the individual work of the players, the practice of the team, how to throw the ball, with illustrations and many valuable hints. Price 10 cents.

No. 199—Equestrian Polo.

Compiled by H. L. Fitzpatrick of the New York Sun. Illustrated with portraits of leading players, and contains most useful information for polo players. Price 10 cents.

No. 271—Spalding's Official Roque Guide.

The official publication of the National Roque Association of America. Contains a description of the courts and their construction, diagrams, illustrations, rules and valuable information. Price 10 cents.

No. 138—Spalding's Official Croquet Guide.

Contains directions for playing, diagrams of important strokes, description of grounds, instructions for the beginner, terms used in the game, and the official playing rules. Price 10 cents.

No. 341—How to Bowl.

The contents include: diagrams of effective deliveries; hints to beginners; how to score; official rules; spares, how they are made; rules for cocked hat, quintet, cocked hat and feather, battle game, etc. Price 10 cents.

No. 248—Archery.

A new and up-to-date book on this fascinating pastime. The several varieties of archery; instructions for shooting; how to select implements; how to score; and a great deal of interesting information. Illustrated. Price 10 cents.

No. 194—Racquets, Squash-Racquets and Court Tennis.

How to play each game is thoroughly explained, and all the difficult strokes shown by special photographs taken especially for this book. Contains the official rules for each game. Price 10 cents.

No. 167—Quoits.

Contains a description of the plays used by experts and the official rules. Illustrated. Price 10 cents.

No. 170—Push Ball.

This book contains the official rules and a sketch of the game; illustrated. Price 10 cents.

No. 13—How to Play Hand Ball.

By the world's champion, Michael Egan. Every play is thoroughly explained by text and diagram. Illustrated. Price 10 cents.

No. 14—Curling.

A short history of this famous Scottish pastime, with instructions for play, rules of the game, definitions of terms and diagrams of different shots. Price 10 cents.

No. 207—Bowling on the Green; or, Lawn Bowls.

How to construct a green; how to play the game, and the official rules of the Scottish Bowling Association. Illustrated. Price 10 cents.

No. 189—Children's Games.

These games are intended for use at recesses, and all but the team games have been adapted to large classes. Suitable for children from three to eight years, and include a great variety. Price 10 cents.

No. 188—Lawn Games.

Lawn Hockey, Garden Hockey, Hand Tennis, Tether Tennis; also Volley Ball, Parlor Hockey, Badminton, Basket Goal. Price 10 cents.

No. 12—Spalding's Official Athletic Almanac.

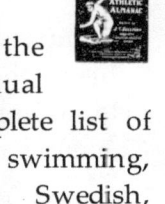

Compiled by J. E. Sullivan, President of the Amateur Athletic Union. The only annual publication now issued that contains a complete list of amateur best-on-records; intercollegiate, swimming, interscholastic, English, Irish, Scotch, Swedish, Continental, South African, Australasian; numerous photos of individual athletes and leading athletic teams. Price 10 cents.

No. 12A—Spalding's Official Athletic Rules.

The A. A. U. is the governing body of athletes in the United States of America, and all games must be held under its rules, which are exclusively published in this handbook, and a copy should be in the hands of every athlete and every club officer in America. Price 10 cents.

No. 27—College Athletics.

M. C. Murphy, the well-known athletic trainer, now with Pennsylvania, the author of this book, has written it especially for the schoolboy and college man, but it is invaluable for the athlete who wishes to excel in any branch of athletic sport; profusely illustrated. Price 10 cents.

No. 182—All-Around Athletics.

Gives in full the method of scoring the All-Around Championship; how to train for the All-Around Championship. Illustrated. Price 10 cents.

No. 156—Athlete's Guide.

Full instructions for the beginner, telling how to sprint, hurdle, jump and throw weights, general hints on training; valuable advice to beginners and important A. A. U. rules and their explanations, while the pictures comprise many scenes of champions in action. Price 10 cents.

No. 273—The Olympic Games at Athens.

A complete account of the Olympic Games of 1906, at Athens, the greatest International Athletic Contest ever held. Compiled by J. E. Sullivan, Special United States Commissioner to the Olympic Games. Price 10 cents.

No. 87—Athletic Primer.

Edited by J. E. Sullivan, Ex-President of the Amateur Athletic Union. Tells how to organize an athletic club, how to conduct an athletic meeting, and gives rules for the government of athletic meetings; contents also include directions for laying out athletic grounds, and a very instructive article on training. Price 10 cents.

No. 252—How to Sprint.

Every athlete who aspires to be a sprinter can study this book to advantage. Price 10 cents.

No. 255—How to Run 100 Yards.

By J. W. Morton, the noted British champion. Many of Mr. Morton's methods of training are novel to American athletes, but his success is the best tribute to their worth. Illustrated. Price 10 cents.

No. 174—Distance and Cross-Country Running.

By George Orton, the famous University of Pennsylvania runner. The quarter, half, mile, the longer distances, and cross-country running and steeplechasing, with instructions for training; pictures of leading athletes in action, with comments by the editors. Price 10 cents.

No. 259—Weight Throwing.

Probably no other man in the world has had the varied and long experience of James S. Mitchel, the author, in the weight throwing department of athletics. The book gives valuable information not only for the novice, but for the expert as well. Price 10 cents.

No. 246—Athletic Training for Schoolboys.

By Geo. W. Orton. Each event in the intercollegiate programme is treated of separately. Price 10 cents.

No. 55—Official Sporting Rules.

Contains rules not found in other publications for the government of many sports; rules for wrestling, shuffleboard, snowshoeing, professional racing, pigeon shooting, dog racing, pistol and revolver shooting, British water polo rules, Rugby foot ball rules. Price 10 cents.

No. 331—Schoolyard Athletics.

By J. E. Sullivan, Ex-President Amateur Athletic Union and member of Board of Education of Greater New York. An invaluable handbook for the teacher and the pupil. Gives a systematic plan for conducting school athletic contests and instructs how to prepare for the various events. Illustrated. Price 10 cents.

No. 317—Marathon Running.

A new and up-to-date book on this popular pastime. Contains pictures of the leading Marathon runners, methods of training, and best times made in various Marathon events. Price 10 cents.

ATHLETIC AUXILIARIES.

No. 339—Official Intercollegiate A. A. A. Handbook.

Contains constitution, by-laws, and laws of athletics; records from 1876 to date. Price 10 cents.

No. 308—Official Handbook New York Interscholastic Athletic Association.

Contains the Association's records, constitution and by-laws and other information. Price 10 cents.

No. 302—Official Y. M. C. A. Handbook.

Contains the official rules governing all sports under the jurisdiction of the Y. M. C. A., official Y. M. C. A. scoring tables, pentathlon rules, pictures of leading Y. M. C. A. athletes. Price 10 cents.

No. 313—Official Handbook of the Public Schools Athletic League.

Edited by Dr. C. Ward Crampton, director of physical education in the Public Schools of Greater New York. Illustrated. Price 10 cents.

No. 314—Official Handbook Girls' Branch of the Public Schools Athletic League.

The official publication. Contains: constitution and by-laws, list of officers, donors, founders, life and annual members, reports and illustrations. Price 10 cents.

No. 177—How to Swim.

Will interest the expert as well as the novice; the illustrations were made from photographs especially posed, showing the swimmer in clear water; a valuable feature is the series of "land drill" exercises for the beginner. Price 10 cents.

No. 296—Speed Swimming.

By Champion C. M. Daniels of the New York Athletic Club team, holder of numerous American records, and the best swimmer in America qualified to write on the subject. Any boy should be able to increase his speed in the water after reading Champion Daniels' instructions on the subject. Price 10 cents.

No. 128—How to Row.

By E. J. Giannini, of the New York Athletic Club, one of America's most famous amateur oarsmen and champions. Shows how to hold the oars, the finish of the stroke and other valuable information. Price 10 cents.

No. 23—Canoeing.

Paddling, sailing, cruising and racing canoes and their uses; with hints on rig and management; the choice of a canoe; sailing canoes, racing regulations; canoeing and camping. Fully illustrated. Price 10 cents.

No. 209—How to Become a Skater.

Contains advice for beginners; how to become a figure skater, showing how to do all the different tricks of the best figure skaters. Pictures of prominent skaters and numerous diagrams. Price 10 cents.

No. 282—Official Roller Skating Guide.

Directions for becoming a fancy and trick roller skater, and rules for roller skating. Pictures of prominent trick skaters in action. Price 10 cents.

No. 178—How to Train for Bicycling.

Gives methods of the best riders when training for long or short distance races; hints on training. Revised and up-to-date in every particular. Price 10 cents.

No. 140—Wrestling.

Catch-as-catch-can style. Seventy illustrations of the different holds, photographed especially and so described that anybody can with little effort learn every one. Price 10 cents.

No. 18—Fencing.

By Dr. Edward Breck, of Boston, editor of The Swordsman, a prominent amateur fencer. A book that has stood the test of time, and is universally acknowledged to be a standard work. Illustrated. Price 10 cents.

No. 162—Boxing Guide.

Contains over 70 pages of illustrations showing all the latest blows, posed especially for this book under the supervision of a well-known instructor of boxing, who makes a specialty of teaching and knows how to impart his knowledge. Price 10 cents.

No. 165—The Art of Fencing

By Regis and Louis Senac, of New York, famous instructors and leading authorities on the subject. Gives in detail how every move should be made. Price 10 cents.

No. 236—How to Wrestle.

The most complete and up-to-date book on wrestling ever published. Edited by F. R. Toombs, and devoted principally to special poses and illustrations by George Hackenschmidt, the "Russian Lion." Price 10 cents.

No. 102—Ground Tumbling.

Any boy, by reading this book and following the instructions, can become proficient. Price 10 cents.

No. 289—Tumbling for Amateurs.

Specially compiled for amateurs by Dr. James T. Gwathmey. Every variety of the pastime explained by text and pictures, over 100 different positions being shown. Price 10 cents.

No. 191—How to Punch the Bag.

The best treatise on bag punching that has ever been printed. Every variety of blow used in training is shown and explained, with a chapter on fancy bag punching by a well-known theatrical bag puncher. Price 10 cents.

No. 200—Dumb-Bells.

The best work on dumb-bells that has ever been offered. By Prof. G. Bojus, of New York. Contains 200 photographs. Should be in the hands of every teacher and pupil of physical culture, and is invaluable for home exercise. Price 10 cents.

No. 143—Indian Clubs and Dumb-Bells.

By America's amateur champion club swinger, J. H. Dougherty. It is clearly illustrated, by which any novice can become an expert. Price 10 cents.

No. 262—Medicine Ball Exercises.

A series of plain and practical exercises with the medicine ball, suitable for boys and girls, business and professional men, in and out of gymnasium. Price 10 cents.

No. 29—Pulley Weight Exercises.

By Dr. Henry S. Anderson, instructor in heavy gymnastics, Yale gymnasium. In conjunction with a chest machine anyone with this book can become perfectly developed. Price 10 cents.

No. 233—Jiu Jitsu.

Each move thoroughly explained and illustrated with numerous full-page pictures of Messrs. A. Minami and K. Koyama, two of the most famous exponents of the art of Jiu Jitsu, who posed especially for this book. Price 10 cents.

No. 166—How to Swing Indian Clubs.

By Prof. E. B. Warman. By following the directions carefully anyone can become an expert. Price 10 cents.

No. 326—Professional Wrestling.

A book devoted to the catch-as-catch-can style; illustrated with half-tone pictures showing the different holds used by Frank Gotch, champion catch-as-catch-can wrestler of the world. Posed by Dr. Roller and Charles Postl. By Ed. W. Smith, Sporting Editor of the Chicago American. Price 10 cents.

No. 104—The Grading of Gymnastic Exercises.

By G. M. Martin. A book that should be in the hands of every physical director of the Y. M. C. A., school, club, college, etc. Price 10 cents.

No. 214—Graded Calisthenics and Dumb-Bell Drills.

For years it has been the custom in most gymnasiums of memorizing a set drill, which was never varied. Consequently the beginner was given the same kind and amount as the older member. With a view to giving uniformity the present treatise is attempted. Price 10 cents.

No. 254—Barnjum Bar Bell Drill.

Edited by Dr. R. Tait McKenzie, Director Physical Training, University of Pennsylvania. Profusely illustrated. Price 10 cents.

No. 158—Indoor and Outdoor Gymnastic Games.

A book that will prove valuable to indoor and outdoor gymnasiums, schools, outings and gatherings where there are a number to be amused. Price 10 cents.

No. 124—How to Become a Gymnast.

By Robert Stoll, of the New York A. C., the American champion on the flying rings from 1885 to 1892. Any boy can easily become proficient with a little practice. Price 10 cents.

No. 287—Fancy Dumb Bell and Marching Drills.

All concede that games and recreative exercises during the

adolescent period are preferable to set drills and monotonous movements. These drills, while designed primarily for boys, can be used successfully with girls and men and women. Profusely illustrated. Price 10 cents.

No. 327—Pyramid Building Without Apparatus.

By W. J. Cromie, Instructor of Gymnastics, University of Pennsylvania. With illustrations showing many different combinations. This book should be in the hands of all gymnasium instructors. Price 10 Cents.

No. 328—Exercises on the Parallel Bars.

By W. J. Cromie. Every gymnast should procure a copy of this book. Illustrated with cuts showing many novel exercises. Price 10 cents.

No. 329—Pyramid Building with Chairs, Wands and Ladders.

By W. J. Cromie. Illustrated with half-tone photographs showing many interesting combinations. Price 10 cents.

GYMNASTIC AUXILIARY.

No. 333—Official Handbook Inter-Collegiate Association Amateur Gymnasts of America.

Edited by P. R. Carpenter, Physical Director Amherst College. Contains pictures of leading teams and individual champions, official rules governing contests, records. Price 10 cents.

No. 161—Ten Minutes' Exercise for Busy Men.

By Dr. Luther Halsey Gulick, Director of Physical Training in the New York Public Schools. A concise and complete course of physical education. Price 10 cents.

No. 208—Physical Education and Hygiene.

This is the fifth of the Physical Training series, by Prof. E. B. Warman (see Nos. 142, 149, 166, 185, 213, 261, 290). Price 10 cents.

No. 149—The Care of the Body.

A book that all who value health should read and follow its instructions. By Prof. E. B. Warman, the well-known lecturer and authority on physical culture. Price 10 cents.

No. 142—Physical Training Simplified.

By Prof. E. B. Warman. A complete, thorough and practical book where the whole man is considered—brain and body. Price 10 cents.

No. 261—Tensing Exercises.

By Prof. E. B. Warman. The "Tensing" or "Resisting" system of muscular exercises is the most thorough, the most complete, the most satisfactory, and the most fascinating of systems. Price 10 cents.

No. 185—Health Hints.

By Prof. E. B. Warman. Health influenced by insulation; health influenced by underwear; health influenced by color; exercise. Price 10 cents.

No. 213—285 Health Answers.

By Prof. E. B. Warman. Contents: ventilating a bedroom; ventilating a house; how to obtain pure air; bathing; salt water baths at home; a substitute for ice water; to cure insomnia, etc., etc. Price 10 cents.

No. 238—Muscle Building.

By Dr. L. H. Gulick. A complete treatise on the correct method of acquiring strength. Illustrated. Price 10 cents.

No. 234—School Tactics and Maze Running.

A series of drills for the use of schools. Edited by Dr. Luther Halsey Gulick. Price 10 cents.

No. 325—Twenty-Minute Exercises.

By Prof. E. B. Warman, with chapters on "How to Avoid Growing Old," and "Fasting: Its Objects and Benefits." Price 10 cents.

No. 285—Health by Muscular Gymnastics.

With hints on right living. By W. J. Cromie. If one will practice the exercises and observe the hints therein contained, he will be amply repaid for so doing. Price 10 cents.

No. 288—Indigestion Treated by Gymnastics.

By W. J. Cromie. If the hints therein contained are observed and the exercises faithfully performed great relief will be experienced. Price 10 cents.

No. 290—Get Well; Keep Well.

By Prof. E. B. Warman, author of a number of books in the Spalding Athletic Library on physical training. Price 10 cents.

No. 330—Physical Training for the School and Class Room.

Edited by G. R. Borden, Physical Director of the Y. M. C. A., Easton, Pa. A book that is for practical work in the school room. Illustrated. Price 10 cents.

A. G. SPALDING

From Photograph
Taken in San Francisco
in November, 1879

Ground Tumbling

BY

HENRY WALTER WORTH

Formerly Physical Director of Armour Institute of
Technology Chicago

PUBLISHED BY THE
AMERICAN SPORTS PUBLISHING COMPANY
21 WARREN STREET, NEW YORK

INTRODUCTION

❧

Oh, do you remember, how, when a small boy in the country, in the months of April, May, June, July, August and September (it mattered little what time of the year it was, just so the ice was out of the water), you used to run to the river at a "twelve-second gait," make two simple twists of the wrist, thereby removing a waist and pair of trousers, and plunge into the water with speed equalled only by the rapidity with which you say your prayers on a cold night? Of course you do. Great fun, was it not? I used to think there was nothing like it. I could not get into the water quick enough. That was before I learned to turn the "back" and the "flip," however.

After I learned to turn the back and forward somersault, when I was about eleven years old, I would linger on the bank, or soft sandy beach, "tumbling," until I saw the other boys coming out to dress, then I would dive in, swim a few strokes, just to say I had been in swimming, come out and dress with the rest.

Like the proverbial "Wandering Willie," the water lost much of its charm for me after I found what royal fun the turning and twisting on the bank afforded. I have wondered many times if the Almighty, when He created beaches like Manhattan, Rockaway and Nantasket, making them slope gently down to the water, and put the soft, but not too soft, yielding sand there, if He did not think how admirable they would be to "tumble" on.

Any one who has experienced the pleasure of a few "backs," "flips," "snap-ups," etc., on the soft sand, immediately after donning the light bathing suit, will agree with me that it is "great fun." And he who has never been taught, never practiced any acrobatic work, I hope will begin "easy" at first; a few simple feats and practice carefully every opportunity he has.

I am sure whoever takes an interest, tries, and advances as far as the "round-off," "flip" and "back," will feel fully repaid for all the time passed in learning. He will find so many opportunities of performing, and it will be a means of great pleasure to himself, if not to his friends.

Many of the acts can be performed in the parlor or in a very small space. However, they should never be *practiced* in the parlor.

Now a few words upon the benefits, physical and mental, derived from practicing tumbling.

An expert tumbler has an everlasting faculty of always landing on his feet. If thrown from a horse, street car or carriage, like a cat that is dropped from a window, and the man who strikes a match on the sole of his boot, he always lights on his feet. There is a sort of wriggle or twist that a man who has practiced tumbling long can make in the air that will invariably bring him down feet first.

The mental benefit is derived from the pleasure found in practicing, as all recreation is a mental benefit. I feel that all I could preach, say or sing about the benefit of any certain exercise would be feeble indeed. Boys and young men—and they are the ones who will probably be most interested in this book—are not appealed to by advice on "what they ought to do." They will never practice any of the feats described in this book for the good it will do them. They know that plenty of sleep is good for them, and they know that tobacco is bad for them; but it makes no difference.

This book is intended more for the boy who wishes to learn but does not know just where and how to begin. What we all need in this world is encouragement. I should like to encourage every boy who wishes to learn. Don't be discouraged because it takes you so long to learn the handspring; when that is once learned, the other acts will be easier.

Do you remember the comparative lines used by a baking powder company in advertising their baking powder? There was the long line reaching nearly across the page, representing this firm's powder, "Absolutely Pure." Then there was the next line, not as long, representing some other firm's powder—not as long a line, and not so pure a powder. Then there were other lines along down the list, shorter and shorter, until the last, which was only about an eighth of an inch long. Now, I think these lines might serve as an excellent illustration of the length of time it will require one to learn the different feats. Let the long line represent the length of time it takes to acquire the first trick; the practice for the first trick will help you with the second, the second with the third, and so on, so that when you have practiced and learned many feats the time required to learn each will grow shorter and shorter, although the acts grow harder.

This rule will apply to all athletic and gymnastic work as well as to tumbling.

To boys who are apt to get discouraged I love to tell of a boy I knew in Chicago. He was far below the average in natural ability when I first knew him—awkward and clumsy—but he became interested in gymnastic work and kept "everlastingly at it." He fairly lived in the gymnasium. As a result of this faithful labor, in less than three months' time he participated in a gymnastic exhibition, turning a forward somersault through a blazing hoop.

Practice, don't be discouraged! You will probably never become as great an acrobat as one of the Nelson Brothers, but you will certainly find great pleasure and accomplish some good results by Ground Tumbling.

THE AUTHOR.

DIRECTIONS

❧

1. The Switch.

This is an act which is easily performed and affords much amusement for spectators. Stand in an erect position with hands hanging at sides, spring up a foot-and-a-half from the ground and give a quick jerk or switch with the body and come down facing in the opposite direction. Do not jump around. The turn is made by a twist of the body, not with the feet or legs.

No. 2. The Sitdown.

2. *The Sit Down.*

Stand with the feet about one foot apart, bend over, keeping the legs perfectly straight, until the finger tips nearly touch the toes, then fall back to a sitting position on the floor. Do not bend the knees. If performed correctly this can be done on a very hard floor without hurting the performer in the least. (See illustration.)

3. The Back Roll.

Performed the same as No. 2, only instead of stopping at the sitting position the performer rolls back on the shoulders and head, and with the use of the hands comes to a standing position on feet.

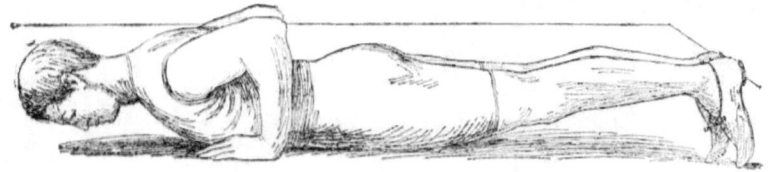

No. 4. The Fish Flop.

4. The Fish Flop.

Lie on stomach, feet close together with the toes touching the floor. Place hands on sides, near ribs, flop over onto back with help of hands and feet, keeping the body perfectly rigid. (See illustration.)

5. The Front Roll.

Stand with heels close together, toes turned out. Bend over, place hands on floor about one foot apart and about a foot-and-a-half in front of feet, bend head in toward body and touch the back of head on floor between hands and, with a push from the feet, roll over on back and up onto feet again. "Curl up" in doing this act. Bring feet well under body.

6. The Cart Wheel.

Stand erect, throw left hand hard down on the floor, about two feet from the left foot, follow with the right hand, two feet from the left hand, then the right foot down about two feet from the right hand, and so on. The feet and hands should be placed as nearly on a straight line as possible. Arms and legs moving like the spokes in a wheel, hence the name.

7. The Round-off.

This may be done with either running or standing start. Strike hands on ground in front of feet, letting the left strike a little before the right, as in the cart-wheel. Place them about ten inches apart, at the same time swing the body over and around, so as to land in a sitting position directly opposite the one in starting.

8. The Handspring.

Possibly the most common acrobatic feat. May be done from running or standing start; strike hands hard on the ground, turn head under and in, throw feet over head and as they begin to come down give a hard spring or push up with the hands, curling feet down and back under body and coming to standing position, facing the same way as when starting.

9. The One-hand Handspring.

Same as No. 8, except that but one hand is used. The weight of the body should be brought well over the hand used.

No. 10. THE HEADSPRING.

10. The Headspring.

Instructions same as for No. 8, only the spring is made from the head instead of the hands. (See illustration.)

No. 11. The Snap Up.

11. The Snap Up.

Lie on back, carry feet up and back over head so that the toes nearly touch the ground, bearing the weight on the back of head, neck and shoulders. The hands should be placed on the ground near shoulders and neck. Give a quick hard whip with the feet and legs over toward first position and a hard snap or push up with the neck, shoulders and hands. With a little practice it can be done without the aid of the hands. It is a pretty act and a good "finish" to every act ending with a fall on the back. (See illustration.)

12. The Elephant Walk.

A comical contortion act. Place hands on floor in front of feet as near to toes as possible. Do not bend the knees. Walk.

13. The Long Dive or Lion's Leap.

This is a long dive made on the mats or some soft place, much as one dives into the water. Take a short run, strike both feet at the same time on a spot about five feet from the mat, make a dive toward the centre of the mat striking first the hands, then the head (which should be well turned down and under), allowing the force of the dive to be about equally divided between the hands, neck, head and shoulders. Curl up well as in No. 5.

14. The Hop Over Hand and Foot.

Grasp left foot with right hand, with thumb of right hand under great toe joint; fingers of right hand over top of toes with backs of fingers up. Jump over hand and foot with right foot. The point to be observed in performing this trick is to keep the right hand and left foot perfectly still while jumping with the right. If moved, they are apt to trip the foot when jumping. This is excellent practice in developing quickness in handling the feet, which is an important factor in tumbling.

15. The Hop Back.

Jump back to original position from finish of No. 14. Try the same trick with both feet over and back.

16. The Jump Over Stick in Hands.

Practice this with a cane or rattan that can be bent down while jumping over. Grasp stick with ordinary grasp, hands placed as far apart as the width of shoulders. Jump over stick between hands, keeping stick in hands. Jump back.

17. *The Jump Over Hat.*

Same as No. 16, except jump is made over hat held in hands.

18. The Jump Over Razor-Blade.

This should never be practiced until the performer can successfully jump over short lead pencil held in hands. It is a "stage trick" that takes well and usually makes a hit. It should be done with a razor-blade so dull that if struck with the feet it would do no harm. Hold the blade of the razor in the hands so loosely that if tripped upon by toes it would easily slip from hands without injury.

No. 19. THE JUMP
OVER HANDS.

19. The Jump Over Hands.

This is one of the prettiest and most difficult acts that is performed. Entwine the fingers together and jump through the arms and over the hands. It may take months of practice to get this feat, but, when once learned, the legs will be so supple and quick that nearly all other acrobatic feats will come easier in consequence. (See illustration.)

20. The Twist Handspring.

Performed the same as No. 8, only, after touching the hands, the body gives a quick turn or twist to the right or left so as to finish the act facing in position used in starting.

21. The Twist Snap-Up.

Same as No. 11, only the body gives a quick turn or twist to the right or left after the shoulders leave the ground so that the finish is made opposite the position taken in starting.

22. The Cradle.

First do the snap-up, No. 11, and immediately after landing fall back onto the shoulders, neck, head and hands as in the snap-up, then snap back to feet and continue to rock back and forth.

23. *The Kicking Jackass.*

Stand with heels close together, jump onto hands, with the feet carried well back and the back arched. Then spring (not fall) back to the feet from the hands and continue the movement. Be sure that the feet leave and strike the ground together, also the hands. Do not "crow-hop," that is, don't strike first one foot and then the other, a sort of "ker-flap," "pit-pat" sound.

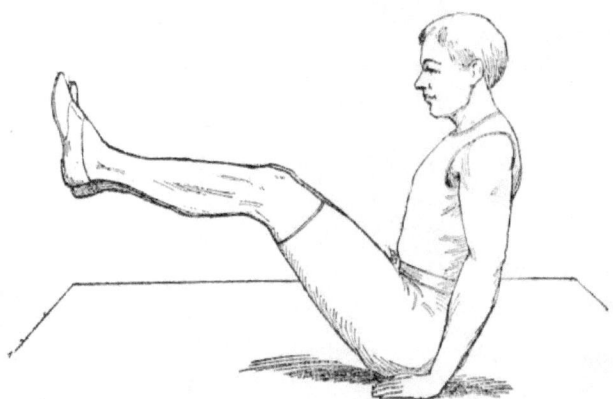

No. 24. THE CURL.

24. The Curl.

Stand erect, fall slowly forward on the hands, keeping the body perfectly straight. Break the force of the fall by letting the arms bend slightly, but straighten them immediately. Curl up, bringing the knees well up toward the chin and carry the feet through between the hands, not letting them touch the floor; extend legs in front of arms, curl up again, carry feet back through hands and straighten into the "handstand." This is a difficult feat, but it may be practiced with perfect safety. It is excellent practice for developing the muscles of the stomach and abdomen. (See illustration.)

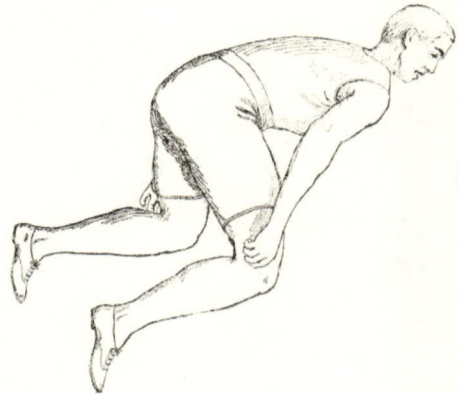

No. 25. RUNNING FORWARD
SOMERSAULT.

25. Running Forward Somersault.

Take a quick run of about twenty yards, strike both feet together on the mat or floor. Jump well into the air, duck the head down and in, and try to describe a half circle through the air, with the feet landing in a position, the same direction as when starting. It is well to practice this over a very soft place, having a board or some hard object to turn from and land into hay, shavings, soft sand, sawdust or tan-bark. When one has a soft place on which to practice he should go at it boldly; he will then be less apt to jar himself. A quick hard run is the important thing, and a leap of about five feet should be made before striking the take-off. (See illustration.)

26. The Back Somersault.

This is done from a standing position. Get two men to hold you up while trying. The "lungers" that are generally used in the gymnasium—"coward-strap" they are called—may be used with perfect safety. However, I think the best kind of strap is a long strong towel.

Stand firmly with the heels about four inches apart, spring up as high as possible, throw the head back and down and try to describe a half circle with the feet landing in a position facing the same way as when starting. This should be performed with a "cut," that is when the feet get well over the head catch the legs back of the knees and pull them down under the body. The way of using the hands in performing the back somersault will gradually come to the performer with practice.

27. The Flip.

Sometimes called "Back Handspring." Should be practiced over a moderately soft place. Stand with the back to the mat. Sink down so that knees come within a foot of the floor in front of feet. Throw the hands and head back. Strike hands on floor, about six inches apart, in a position such as is held while walking on hands. Do not let the head touch the ground. Then throw the feet up over the head and hands, describing a half circle, finishing facing the same way as when starting. Use the stomach and abdomen muscles when performing this act. Do not let the feet leave the ground until the hands are firmly placed.

28. The Twister.

This is No. 26, the back somersault, with a half turn to the right or left, so that the finish is made facing in an opposite position from the position in starting. It is well in practising this act to try and turn just a little at first, then an inch further, and so on until the complete half turn is made.

29. The Twist Flip.

Same as No. 27, the "flip," only a half turn is made from the hands so as to finish facing in an opposite direction from that taken when starting.

30. The Spotter.

This is the back somersault turned in such a way as to finish with the feet in the same spot they were when starting. It is best acquired by trying to make each finish nearer and nearer to the starting position.

31. The Gainer.

Same as No. 30, except that the finish is made with the feet striking in front of the starting position.

32. The Tuck-up.

This is a high back somersault performed without the "cut."
It is usually done as a finish to a succession of "flips."

33. The Standing Forward.

This is the forward somersault performed without a run. To do this one must jump high into the air, turning as he would in the running forward and "cut" by catching the legs in front, just above the ankles, and drawing them under the ankles. It is a difficult act.

34. The Half Forward.

The first part of this act is performed as in No. 25, only, instead of having the feet describe a circle over the head, they stop in the air above head, and the landing is made on the hands. It is, in fact, a sort of jump or dive on the hands and stand there.

No. 35. THE HALF BACK.

35. The Half Back.

Like No. 26, only the finish is made onto the hands and the body balanced there. Instead of turning all the way around, jump back onto the hands and stand there. (See illustration.)

This concludes the article on "single acts." In the next chapter I will describe how the acts can be suitably combined. A clever performer can make combinations other than these. In fact, there are an endless variety of combinations that can be made with the acts here described. Space will not allow of a longer or more thorough description.

COMBINATIONS

36.   A succession of No. 5.

37.   A combination of Nos. 2 and 3.

38.   A succession of No. 6.

39.   A combination of Nos. 2, 3, 4 and 11.

40.   A combination of Nos. 11 and 8.

41.   A combination of Nos. 10 and 8.

42.   A succession of No. 8.

43.   A succession of No. 11.

44.   A succession of No. 10.

45.   A combination of Nos. 7, 2 and 3.

46.   A combination of Nos. 7, 2, 3, 4 and 11.

47.   A combination of Nos. 7, 2, 3, 4, 11 and 23.

48.   A succession of No. 21.

49.   A combination of Nos. 8 and 33.

50.   No. 13 through hoop.

51.   A combination of Nos. 7 and 26.

52.   A combination of Nos. 7 and 27.

53.   A combination of Nos. 23 and 26.

54.   A combination of Nos. 24 and 33.

55.   A combination of Nos. 7, 27 and 26.

56.   A combination of Nos. 7, 27, 26 and 33.

57.   A combination of No. 7 and a succession of Nos. 27
        and 32.

58. A succession of Nos. 8 and 34, then a succession of No. 27.

59. A combination of No. 7, a succession of Nos. 27 and 28, then a succession of Nos. 27 and 32.

Home Apparatus

"It is not so important to have big muscles as it is to have good digestion; it is not so important to have powerful muscles as it is, to have a strong, regular heart; it is not so important to have great skill with one's muscles as to have good lungs and kidneys." —*Extract from Spalding Athletic Library No. 161 —"Ten Minutes' Exercise for Busy Men."*

The value of a few minutes' exercise daily with scientific and properly designed apparatus, is rapidly becoming apparent to the vast number of business men who find it simply impossible to take regular outdoor exercise.

Spalding Gold Medal Indian Clubs

Model, material and finish as perfect as the most complete and up-to-date factory can make them.

Natural Color, Lathe Polished, High Finish,

Spalding Gold Medal Indian Clubs are made of selected first grade clear maple, in two popular models and are perfect in balance. Each club bears fac-simile of the Spalding Gold Medal. Each pair is wrapped in paper bag.

MODEL E

Model
E

Weights specified are for each club.

½	lb.	Model E.	Pair,	$ .60
¾	lb.	Model E.	Pair,	.60
1	lb.	Model E.	Pair,	.70
1½	lb.	Model E.	Pair,	.80
2	lb.	Model E.	Pair,	**1.00**
3	lb.	Model E.	Pair,	**1.20**

Mo(
B

MODEL B

Weights specified are for each club.

½	lb.	Model B.	Pair,	$ .50
¾	lb.	Model B.	Pair,	.50
1	lb.	Model B.	Pair,	.55
1½	lb.	Model B.	Pair,	.60
2	lb.	Model	Pair,	.70

B.

3 lb. Model Pair, **1.00**
B.

Spalding Trade-Mark Indian Clubs

Stained Finish.

The following clubs bear our Trade-Mark, are made of good material, and are far superior in shape and finish to the best clubs of other makes. Furnished in two popular models. Each pair wrapped in paper bag.

MODEL ES

Weights specified are for each club.

Model
ES

Mo
BS

½	lb.	Model ES.	Pair,	**$** **.35**
¾	lb.	Model ES.	Pair,	**.35**
1	lb.	Model ES.	Pair,	**.40**
1½	lb.	Model ES.	Pair,	**.50**
2	lb.	Model ES.	Pair,	**.60**
3	lb.	Model ES.	Pair,	**.70**

MODEL BS

*Weights specified are for each
club.*

½	lb.	Model BS.	Pair,	$ .30
¾	lb.	Model BS.	Pair,	.30
1	lb.	Model BS.	Pair,	.35
1½	lb.	Model BS.	Pair,	.45
2	lb.	Model BS.	Pair,	.55
3	lb.	Model BS.	Pair,	.65

Spalding Exhibition Clubs

Handsomely finished in ebonite and made for
exhibition and stage purposes. The clubs are
hollow, with a large body, and although
extremely light, represent a club weighing three
pounds or more.

No.
A

No
AA

No. **A.** Ebonite finish.   **$3.50**

No. **AA.** With German Silver
Bands.   Pair, **$5.00**

No. 1

Spalding Indian Club and Dumb Bell Hangers

Made of iron and nicely japanned.

No. **1.** For Indian Clubs or Dumb Bells.

Per pair, **16c.**

No. **1M.** For Indian Clubs or Dumb Bells, mounted on oak strips.

Per pair, **25c.**

Spalding Gold Medal Wood Dumb Bells

There is Skill Used in Turning Spalding Dumb Bells. They
Feel Right
Because They Are So

Natural Color, Lathe Polished, High Finish

Model A

Spalding Gold Medal Dumb Bells are made of selected first
grade clear maple, and are perfect in balance. Each bell bears
fac-simile of the Spalding Gold Medal. Each pair is wrapped
in paper bag. Weights specified are for each bell.

	½ lb.	¾ lb.	1 lb.	1½ lb.	2 lb.
Pair,	**40c.**	**45c.**	**50c.**	**55c.**	**65c.**

Spalding Trade-Mark Wood Dumb Bells

Stained Finish

Model AW

Spalding Trade-Mark quality. Made of good material and superior in shape and finish to the best wood dumb bells of other makes. Each pair wrapped in paper bag. Weights specified are for each bell.

	½ lb.	¾ lb.	1 lb.	1½ lb.	2 lb.
Pair,	**30c.**	**30c.**	**35c.**	**45c.**	**55c.**

Spalding Iron Dumb Bells

Made on approved models, nicely balanced and finished in black enamel.

Sizes 2 to 40 pounds,	**6c.**
Over 40 pounds,	**8c.**
Bar Bells, any weight, wrought iron handles, any length made specially.	Pound, **10c.**

Spalding Nickel-Plated Dumb Bells

Nickel-plated
and polished.

1N. 1 lb.   **$ .25**

2N. 2 lb.	.50
3N. 3 lb.	.65
4N. 4 lb.	.75
5N. 5 lb.	1.00

Spalding Nickel-Plated Dumb Bells

With Rubber Bands

Nickel-plated
and polished.

1B. 1 lb.	$ .65
2B. 2 lb.	.75
3B. 3 lb.	1.00
4B. 4 lb.	1.15
5B. 5 lb.	1.25

Savage Bar Bell—Especially designed by Dr. Watson L. Savage.

Model S. Has large pear-shaped ends with a flexible hickory shaft ½-inch in diameter, producing a vibratory exercise, similar to that obtained with the French wand.

Per dozen, **$6.00**

Spalding Ash Bar Bells

No. **2.** Selected material, highly polished, 5 feet long.

Per dozen, **$5.00**

Spalding School Wand

No. **3.** 3½ feet long. Made of straight grain maple.

Per dozen, **$1.30**

Spalding Calisthenic Wand

No. **4.** 4½ feet long. 1-inch diameter.

Per dozen, **$1.60**

Home Apparatus

"If a man gets plenty of food, and his digestive apparatus works it up into good rich blood; if the heart is strong and regular so that this good blood goes to all parts of the body with vigor and regularity, and if the respiratory and excretory apparatus is in such good order that this blood is kept pure, the fundamental conditions of health are laid." — "*Extracts from Spalding Athletic Library No. 161.*" — "*Ten Minutes' Exercise for Busy Men.*"

Rational exercise with simple but correct apparatus will enable almost any man to arrive at approximately a correct state of health.

SPALDING IMPROVED MEDICINE BALLS

An excellent form of exercise for business men

Weigh from four to eleven pounds. The covering is of selected tan leather, sewn in the same manner as our foot balls. Quality throughout has been much improved and the balls as now made are extremely durable. The exercise consists of throwing ball to one another, and the catching of it develops the chest, exercises the back, arms, legs; in fact,

112

improves the whole system.

No. **11.** 4-pound Ball.	Each, **$5.00**
No. **12.** 6-pound Ball.	Each, **6.00**
No. **13.** 9-pound Ball.	Each, **7.00**
No. **14.** 11-pound Ball.	Each, **10.00**

Home Apparatus

"One of the aims of physical training is to make exercise interesting and enjoyable. To be beneficial in the highest sense it must be recreative. Particularly is this true of physical exercise for business men. As a class, in their daily work, they are kept on a constant mental strain. Besides, they are, to a large degree, physically inactive. Life becomes too intense, too serious, too sordid. Exercise therefore, for business men, must be largely recreative, relaxing and restful." —*Extract from Spalding Athletic Library, No. 262 —"Exercises with the Medicine Ball."*

SPALDING HAND BALLS

Hand ball, played indoors, will keep base ball players and other athletes in good condition during hard weather when outdoor athletics are out of the question.

The leather-covered hand balls we make are wound by hand, and are the same as those used by the best ball players in this country.

No. **1.** Match, regulation size and weight, leather cover.	Each, **$1.25**

No. **2**. Expert, leather cover.	.85
No. **6**. Rubber, best quality, almost solid.	.40
No. **4**. Amateur, leather cover.	.25
No. **5**. Rubber hand ball.	.25

The Irish Regulation Balls have been improved in quality and will give excellent satisfaction.

RED ACE, IRISH REGULATION red rubber ball.	Each, 50c.
BLACK ACE, IRISH REGULATION black rubber ball.	Each, 50c.

For other balls suitable for Hand Ball Game, see page devoted to Lawn Tennis Balls.

 ## Spalding Hand Ball Gloves and Mitts

No. **A**. Gloves. Best quality glove leather with stitched front and special wrist pad.	Pair, $4.00
No. **B**. Mitts. Lightly padded.	3.00
No. **C**. Gloves. Full fingered.	1.50
No. **D**. Fingerless Gloves.	.75

Sandow's Patent

Spring Grip

Dumb Bells

EUGEN
SANDOW,
Patentee.

A. G. SPALDING & BROS.

SOLE AMERICAN AND CANADIAN
LICENSEES

An entire system of Physical Culture is embraced within the exercises possible with these wonderful dumb bells.

The bells are made in two halves connected by steel springs, the effort necessary in gripping compelling the pupil to continually devote his whole mind to each movement. This concentration of will power on each muscle involved is what is responsible for the great results obtained through properly exercising with them.

Sandow's Patent Spring Grip Dumb Bells

No. 6.
MEN'S

No. **6. MEN'S**. Nickel-plated; fitted with seven steel springs.

Per pair,
$3.00

No. **4. LADIES'**. Nickel-plated; fitted with five steel springs.

Per pair
$2.50

No. **2. BOYS'**. Nickel-plated; fitted with four steel springs.

No. 4.
Per pair LADIES'
$2.00

We include with each pair of Sandow Dumb Bells a chart of exercises by Sandow and full instructions for using. Also a piece of selvyt cloth for keeping dumb bells in good condition.

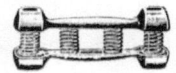

No. 2.
BOYS'

Spalding Home Apparatus

Exercise acts on the health of an individual in the same way as the draught does on the fire in a furnace. Pile on the coal and shut off the draught and you kill the fire. Continue to eat heavy meals and take no exercise and your health will be affected, not because of the food you have eaten so much as on account of the lack of exercise. A little exercise is all that is necessary to keep you in good condition. Some rational, pleasant and interesting exercise, persisted in with regularity and, preferably, with Spalding Home Apparatus, will help you to retain your health.

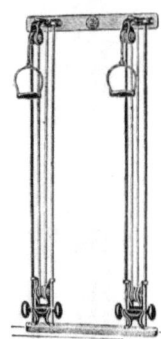

Spalding Chest Weight No. 2

An ideal machine for home use. Well made and easy running. Rods are ⅜-inch coppered spring steel. Bearings are hardened steel cone points running in soft, gray iron, noiseless and durable. Weight carriage packed with felt, good for long wear, but easily removed and replaced when necessary without the use of glue or wedges of any kind. Weight carriage strikes on rubber bumpers. Weights are 5-pound iron dumb-bells, one to each carriage, and may be removed and used as dumb bells. Wall and floor boards are hard wood, nicely finished and stained. All castings heavily japanned. Every part of machine guaranteed free of defect.

No. **2.**   Each.

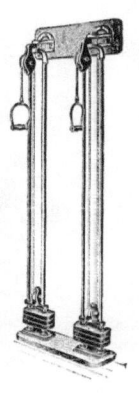

$5.00

Spalding Chest Weight No. 12

We have just added this very well-made machine to our line. Cast iron parts are all nicely *japanned*. The wheels are iron, turned true on centers, and have hardened steel cone point bearings. The guide rods are spring steel, copper-plated. The weight carriage has removable felt bushings, noiseless and durable. Each handle is equipped with 10 lbs. of weights.

No. **12.**   Each,
$10.00

Showing important details of Construction of No. 12 Machine.

The Laflin Friction Rowing Machine

Do not use oil on friction cylinder. If its action is not perfectly smooth a little clear soap rubbed on its surface will properly correct its action. The means used to produce the resistance is a simple friction clutch, which takes instant hold at the commencement of the stroke and retains the pressure till its completion, when it instantly releases it precisely as in a boat. Quickly taken apart without loosening any bolts or screws. Each machine is adjustable to any amount of friction or resistance.

No. **119.** Complete, **$16.00**

Home Apparatus

The apparatus listed in this catalogue is designed particularly for private use; i. e., in homes and private gymnasiums. It retains the same superior marks of quality which distinguish the regular line of gymnasium apparatus manufactured by A. G. Spalding & Bros., but its distinctive design permits it to be sold at a price more in keeping with its use than heretofore obtainable, without any sacrifice of practical value or durability.

Kerns' Rowing Machine

Operated just like rowing a boat

Suitable alike for the Athlete or the ordinary Man or Woman

The ideal boat for home use and training purposes. Used by the leading athletic clubs, colleges and prominent oarsmen of the world, and pronounced the most perfect rowing machine ever produced. Fitted with the Kerns' Patent Roller Seat and Shoes, the shoes having a three-inch adjustment, to suit either a tall or a short person. By turning a thumb-nut the belt can be tightened to any desired degree, and more or less friction thrown into the running parts, imitating the resistance which exists when forcing a row-boat through the water. The weaker sex can use the machine by simply loosening the thumb-nut which reduces the resistance; and on the other hand, by reversing the operation the resistance can be so increased that the strongest athlete can have any amount of resistance. The oars are pivoted in such a way that the operator can handle and turn them the same as he would during the return and feathering motion with a boat oar.

No. 600. Kerns' Patent Single   **Each,**
Scull Rowing Machine.   **$30.00**

Spalding New and Improved Worsted Jerseys

Following sizes carried in stock regularly in all qualities: 28 to 44 inch chest.

Other sizes at an advanced price.

We allow two inches for stretch in all our Jerseys, and sizes are marked accordingly. It is suggested, however, that for very heavy men a size about two inches larger than coat measurement be ordered to insure a comfortable fit.

STOCK COLORS

Jerseys are being used more and more by base ball players, especially for early Spring and late Fall games. The

PLAIN COLORS—The following stock colors are supplied in our worsted jerseys (NOT Nos. 6 or 6X) at regular prices. Other colors to order only in any quality (EXCEPT Nos. 6 and 6X). 25c. each extra.

**Spalding
line
includes a
complete
assortment
of
styles and
qualities.**

Gray
Orange
Black
White
Maroon
Scarlet
Cardinal
Navy Blue
Royal Blue
Columbia Blue
Peacock Blue
Dark Green
Olive Green
Irish Green
Pink
Purple
Yellow
Seal Brown
Old Gold
Drab

No. **1P.** Full regular made; that is, fashioned or knit to exact shape on the machine and then put together by hand, altogether different from cutting them out of a piece of material and sewing them up on a machine as are the majority of garments known as Jerseys. Special quality worsted. Solid stock colors. Each, **$4.50**

No. **10P.** Worsted, fashioned. Solid stock colors, Each, **$3.00**

No. **12P.** Worsted; solid stock colors. Each, **$2.75**

No. **12XB.** Boys' Jersey. Worsted. Furnished in sizes 26 to 36 inches chest measurement only. Solid stock colors only. No special orders. Each, **$2.00**

SPECIAL NOTICE

We will furnish any of the above solid color Jerseys (except Nos. 6 and 6X), with one color body and another color (not striped) collar and cuffs in stock colors only at no extra charge.

Spalding Cotton Jerseys

No. **6.** Cotton, good quality, fashioned, roll collar, full-length sleeves. Colors: Black, Navy Blue, Gray and Maroon only.

Each, **$1.00** Nos. 1P, 10P and 12P

No. **6X.** Cotton, same as No. 6, but with striped sleeves in following combinations only: Navy with White or Red stripe; Black with

Orange or Red stripe;   Each
Maroon with White stripe. $1.25

Woven Letters, Numerals or Designs

We weave into our best grade Jerseys, No. 1P,
Letters, Numerals and Designs in special colors
as desired. Prices quoted on application. Designs submitted.

PRICES SUBJECT TO ADVANCE WITHOUT NOTICE

Spalding Coat Jerseys

Following sizes carried in stock regularly in all qualities: 28 to 44 inch chest. Other sizes at an advanced price.

We allow two inches for stretch in all our Jerseys, and sizes are marked accordingly. It is suggested, however, that for very heavy men a size about two inches larger than coat measurement be ordered to insure a comfortable fit.

STOCK COLORS

Gray
Orange
Black
White
Maroon
Scarlet
Cardinal
Navy
Royal Blue
Columbia Blue
Peacock Blue
Dark Green
Olive Green
Irish Green
Pink
Purple
Yellow
Seal Brown
Old Gold
Drab

PLAIN COLORS—The above stock colors are supplied in our worsted jerseys (NOT Nos. 6 or 6X) at regular prices. Other colors to order only in any quality (EXCEPT Nos. 6 or 6X) 25c. each extra.

STRIPES AND TRIMMINGS—Supplied as specialised in any of the above stock colors (not more than two colors in any garment) at regular prices. Other colors to order only in any quality (EXCEPT Nos. 6 or 6X) 25c. each extra.

Nos. 10C
and 12C

The Spalding Coat Jerseys are made of the same worsted yarn from which we manufacture our better grade Jerseys, Nos. 10P and 12P, and no pains have been spared to turn them out in a well-made and attractive manner. Plain solid stock colors (not striped) or one solid stock color body and sleeves with different stock color solid trimming (not striped) on cuffs, collar and front edging. Pearl buttons.

No. 10CP

	Each.
No. **10C**. Same grade as our No. 10P.	**$3.50**
No. **12C**. Same grade as our No. 12P.	Each. **$3.00**
No. **10CP**. Pockets, otherwise same as No. 10C.	Each, **$4.25**

Nos. 10PW

Spalding Striped and V-Neck Jerseys

Note list of stock colors above

No. 12PV

and 12PW

No. **10**PW. Good quality worsted, same grade as No. 10P. Solid stock color body and sleeves, with 6-inch stock color stripe around body.   Each, **$3.50**

No. **12**PW. Worsted; solid stock color body and sleeves with 6-inch stock color stripe around body.   Each, **$3.00**

No. **10**PX. Good quality worsted, fashioned; solid stock color body, with stock color striped sleeves, usually alternating two inches of same color as body, with narrow stripes of any other stock color.   Each, **$3.50**

No. **12**PV Worsted, solid stock colors, with V-neck instead of full collar as on regular jerseys.   Each, **$3.00**

No. **12**PX. Worsted, solid stock color body, with stock color striped sleeves, usually alternating two inches of same color as body, with narrow stripes of any other stock color.   Each, **$3.00**

Nos. 10PX
and 12PX

SPALDING *Automobile* SWEATER

Collar
Turned Up

Collar
Turned
Down

No. **WJ.** Most satisfactory and
comfortable style for
automobilists; also useful
for training purposes,
reducing weight, tramping
during cold weather,
golfing, shooting,
tobogganing, snowshoeing;
in fact, for every purpose
where a garment is required
to give protection from cold
or inclement weather. High
collar that may be turned

down, changing it into
neatest form of button front
sweater. Highest quality
special heavy weight
worsted. Sizes, 28 to 44   Each,
inches. In stock colors.   **$8.50**

PLAIN COLORS—All Spalding Sweaters are supplied in any of the colors designated, at regular prices. Other colors to order only in any quality, 50c. each garment extra.

SPECIAL NOTICE—We will furnish any of the solid color sweaters with one color body and another color (not striped) collar and cuffs in stock colors only at no extra charge.

N. B.—We designate three shades which are sometimes called RED: These are Scarlet, Cardinal and Maroon. Where RED is specified on order Scarlet will be supplied.

STOCK COLORS

Gray
Orange
Black
White
Maroon
Scarlet
Cardinal
Navy
Royal Blue
Columbia Blue
Peacock Blue
Dark Green
Olive Green
Irish Green
Pink
Purple
Yellow

Seal Brown
Old Gold
Drab

Spalding "Highest Quality" Sweaters

We allow four inches for stretch in all our sweaters, and sizes are marked accordingly. It is suggested, however, that for very heavy men a size about two inches larger than coat measurement be ordered to insure a comfortable fit.

WORSTED SWEATERS. Made of special quality wool, and exceedingly soft and pleasant to wear. They are full fashioned to body and arms and put together by hand, not simply stitched up on a machine as are the majority of garments sold as regular made goods.

All made with 9-inch collars; sizes 28 to 44 inches.

No. **AA.** The proper style for use after heavy exercise, inducing copious perspiration, for reducing weight or getting into condition for athletic contests. Particularly suitable also for Foot Ball and Skating. Heaviest sweater made. In stock colors. Each. **$9.00**

No. **A.** "Intercollegiate." In stock colors. Special weight. **7.00**

No. **B.** Heavy weight. In stock

colors.   6.00

**Front
View**

Spalding Combined Knitted
Muffler and Chest Protector

**Back
View**

No. **M.** Special weight; highest
quality worsted in solid
stock colors to match our   Each,
sweaters.   **$1.25**

**PRICES SUBJECT TO CHANGE
WITHOUT NOTICE**

Shaker Sweater

In Stock
Colors

Sizes 30 to
44 in.

Fills a demand for as heavy a weight as our "Highest
Quality" grade, but at a lower price.

No. **3.** Standard weight,   Each,
slightly lighter than No. B.   **$4.00**

Spalding Vest Collar Sweater

No. **BG.** Best quality worsted, good weight; with extreme open or low neck. In stock colors.   Ea., **$6.00**

SPALDING JACKET SWEATERS

STOCK COLORS PLAIN COLORS—All Spalding Sweaters are supplied in any of the following stock colors at regular prices. Other colors to order only in any quality 50c. each extra.

GRAY
ORANGE
BLACK
WHITE
MAROON
SCARLET
CARDINAL
NAVY BLUE
ROYAL BLUE
COLUMBIA BLUE
PEACOCK BLUE
DARK GREEN
OLIVE GREEN
IRISH GREEN
PINK
PURPLE
YELLOW
SEAL BROWN
OLD GOLD
DRAB

SPECIAL NOTICE—We will furnish any of the solid color sweaters mentioned below with one color body and another color (not striped) collar and cuffs in stock colors only at no extra charge. This does not apply to the No. 3JB Boys' Sweater.

Sizes 28 to 44 inch chest measurement. We allow four inches for stretch in all our sweaters, and sizes are marked accordingly. It is suggested, however, that for very heavy men a size about two inches larger than coat measurement be ordered to insure a comfortable fit.

No. VGP

No. VG.
Showing special trimmed edging and cuffs supplied, if desired, on jacket sweaters at no extra charge.

BUTTON FRONT

No. **VG.** Best quality worsted, heavy weight, pearl buttons. Made in regular stock colors, also in Dark Brown Mixture.   Each, **$7.00**

No. **DJ.** Fine worsted, standard weight, pearl buttons, fine knit edging. Made in regular stock colors, also in Sage Gray.   Each, **$6.00**

No. **3J.** Standard weight wool,

Shaker knit, pearl buttons.
In stock colors.

Each,
$5.00

WITH POCKETS

No. **VGP.** Best quality
worsted, heavy weight,
pearl buttons. In stock
colors. With pocket on
either side and a particularly
convenient and popular
style for golf players.

Each,
$7.50

Spalding Special Base Ball Sweaters

No. CDW

No. 3JB

No. **CDW.** Good quality
worsted, ribbed knit. In
stock colors. Special
trimmed edging and cuffs in
stock colors supplied at no
extra charge.

Each,
$5.50

Boys' Jacket Sweater

No. **3JB.** This is an all wool
jacket sweater, with pearl
buttons; furnished only in
sizes from 30 to 36 inches

chest measurement. In stock
colors.

Each,
$3.50

Spalding Ladies' Sweaters

Knit in the Spalding athletic stitch of best quality long fibre worsted; full fashioned to shape of body on special machine and finished by hand. Cuffs, pocket and edging of special stitch. Good quality pearl buttons. Patch pockets. Attractive in appearance and, being properly made, they fit well and give satisfactory wear. Furnished in regular stock colors.

No. **LDJ.** Ladies' Sweater,
regular button front.

Each,
$8.00

No. **LWJ.** With special
reversible collar, as on our
Men's No. WJ Automobile
Sweater.

Each,
$10.00

The Spalding Official Intercollegiate Foot Ball

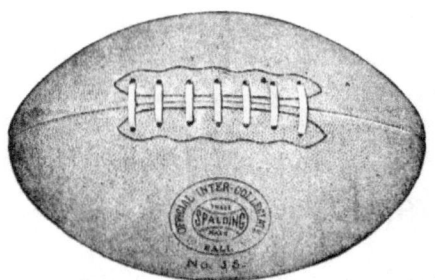

This is the ONLY OFFICIAL COLLEGE FOOT BALL, and is used in every important match played in this country. **Guaranteed absolutely if seal of box is unbroken.** We pack with leather case and guaranteed pure Para rubber bladder (no composition), an inflater, lacing needle and rawhide lace.

No. J5. Complete, $5.00

WE GUARANTEE every Spalding Foot Ball to be perfect in material and workmanship and correct in shape and size when inspected at our factory. If any defect is discovered during the first game in which it is used, or during the first day's practice use, and if returned at once, we will replace same under this guarantee. We do not guarantee against ordinary wear nor against defect in shape or size that is not discovered immediately after the first day's use.

Owing to the superb quality of every Spalding Foot Ball, our customers have grown to expect a season's use of one ball, and at times make unreasonable claims under our guarantee which we will not allow.

A.G. Spalding & Bros

Spalding All-Steel Playground Apparatus

Acknowledged as the Standard. Specified and purchased by
practically all Municipal Park and Playground Commissions
in America.

Correspondence Invited.

Special Plans and
Estimates on Request.

SPALDING PLAYGROUND
APPARATUS IS USED IN

Alameda, Cal.
Allegheny, Pa.
Ashburnham, Mass.
Baltimore, Md.
Bayonne, N. J.
Bloomfield, N. J.
Boston, Mass.

Brooklyn, N. Y.
Bryn Mawr, Pa.
Buffalo, N. Y.
Catskill, N. Y.
Chicago, Ill.
Cincinnati, O.
Cleveland, O.
Dallas, Texas
Dayton, O.
Denver, Col.
Dongan Hills, N. Y.
East Orange, N. J.
Forest Park, Md.
Ft. Plain, N. Y.
Ft. Wayne, Ind.
Galesburg, Ill.
Geneva, N. Y.
Greeley, Col.
Hamilton, Ontario, Can.
Havana, Cuba
Hoboken, N. J.
Jersey City, N. J.
Kansas City, Mo.
Kentfield, Cal.
Lancaster, Pa.
Leavenworth, Kan.
Lexington, Ind.
Lockhart, Ala.
Los Angeles, Cal.
Louisville, Ky.
Lowell, Mass.
Lynn, Mass.
Madison, N. J.
Melrose, Mass.
Meridian, Miss.
Milwaukee, Wis.
Morristown, N. J.
Nashville, Tenn.
Naugatuck, Ct.
Newark, N. J.
New Brunswick, N. J.
New Haven, Ct.

New London, Ct.
New Paltz, N. Y.
New York, N. Y.
Oakland, Cal.
Omaha, Neb.
Orange, N. J.
Oswego, N. Y.
Pasadena, Cal.
Passaic, N. J.
Philadelphia, Pa.
Pittsburgh, Pa.
Pocatello, Idaho
Polk, Pa.
Portland, Me.
Portland, Ore.
Porto Barrios, S. Am.
Pueblo, Col.
Reading, Pa.
Rochester, N. Y.
Rye, N. Y.
Sag Harbor, N. Y.
San Jose, Cal.
Seattle, Wash.
Springfield, Mass.
Somerville, Mass.
St. Louis, Mo.
Summit, N. J.
Utica, N. Y.
Walla Walla, Wash.
Washington, D. C.
Watertown, Mass.
Watervleit, N. Y.
Westfield, Mass.
Wilkes-Barre, Pa.
Winnipeg, Man., Can.
Winthrop, Mass.
Worcester, Mass.
Ypsilanti, Mich.

A. G. SPALDING & BROS., Inc.
Gymnasium and Playground Contract Department

CHICOPEE, MASS.

Spalding "Official National League"

REG. U.S. PAT. OFF.

Ball

Official Ball of the Game for over Thirty Years

Adopted by the National League in 1878, and the only ball used in Championship games since that time. Each ball wrapped in tinfoil, packed in a separate box, and sealed in accordance with the latest League regulations. Warranted to last a full game when used under ordinary conditions.

No. 1. Each, $1.25   **Per Dozen,**

$15.00

Durand-Steel Lockers

Six Lockers
In Double
Tier

Wooden lockers are objectionable, because they attract vermin, absorb odors, can be easily broken into, and are dangerous on account of fire.

Lockers made from wire mesh or expanded metal afford little security, as they can be easily entered with wire cutters. Clothes placed in them become covered with dust, and the lockers themselves present a poor appearance, resembling animal cages.

Some of the 6,000 Durand-Steel Lockers Installed in the
Public Gymnasiums of Chicago. 12′ × 15′ × 42′, Double Tier.

Durand-Steel Lockers are made of finest grade furniture steel and are finished with gloss black, furnace-baked japan (400°), comparable to that used on hospital ware, which will never flake off nor require refinishing, as do paints and enamels.

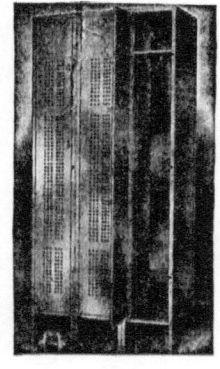

Three Lockers
In Single Tier

148

Durand-Steel Lockers are usually built with doors perforated full length in panel design with sides and backs solid. This prevents clothes in one locker from coming in contact with wet garments in adjoining lockers, while plenty of ventilation is secured by having the door perforated its entire length, but, if the purchaser prefers, we perforate the backs also.

The cost of Durand-Steel Lockers is no more than that of first-class wooden lockers, and they last as long as the building, are sanitary, secure, and, in addition, are fireproof.

THE FOLLOWING STANDARD SIZES ARE THOSE MOST COMMONLY USED:

DOUBLE TIER
12 × 12 × 36 Inch
15 × 15 × 36 Inch
12 × 12 × 42 Inch
15 × 15 × 42 Inch

SINGLE TIER
12 × 12 × 60 Inch
15 × 15 × 60 Inch
12 × 12 × 72 Inch
15 × 15 × 72 Inch

We are handling lockers as a special contract business, and shipment will in every case be made direct from the factory in Chicago. If you will let us know the number of lockers, size and arrangement, we shall be glad to take up, through correspondence, the matter of prices.

PROMPT ATTENTION GIVEN TO ANY COMMUNICATIONS ADDRESSED TO US

A. G. SPALDING & BROS. STORES IN ALL LARGE CITIES

FOR COMPLETE LIST OF STORES SEE INSIDE FRONT COVER OF THIS BOOK

Prices in effect January 5, 1910. Subject to change without notice. For Canadian prices see special Canadian catalogue.

The following selection of items from their latest Catalogue will give an idea of the great variety of ATHLETIC GOODS manufactured by A. G. SPALDING & BROS. SEND FOR A FREE COPY.

Archery

Bags—
  Bat
  Cricket
  Striking
  Uniform
Balls—

Base
Basket
Cricket
Field Hockey
Foot, College
Foot, Rugby
Foot, Soccer
Golf
Hand
Indoor
Medicine
Playground
Squash
Tennis
Volley
Water Polo

Bandages, Elastic

Bathing Suits

Bats—
  Base Ball
  Cricket

Belts

Caps—
  Base Ball
  University
  Water Polo

Chest Weights

Circle, Seven-Foot

Coats, Base Ball

Collars, Swimming

Corks, Running

Covers, Racket

Cricket Goods

Croquet Goods

Discus, Olympic

Dumb Bells

Emblems

Equestrian Polo

Exerciser, Home

Felt Letters

Fencing Sticks

Field Hockey

Flags—
  College
  Foul, Base Ball
  Marking, Golf

Foils, Fencing

Foot Balls—
  Association
  College
  Rugby

Glasses, Base Ball—
  Sun
  Automobile

Gloves—

Base Ball
Boxing
Cricket
Fencing
Foot Ball
Golf
Handball
Hockey, Ice

Glove Softener

Goals—
Basket Ball
Foot Ball
Hockey, Ice

Golf Clubs

Golf Counters

Golfette

Gymnasium, Home

Gymnasium Board

Hammers, Athletic

Hats, University

Head Harness

Health Pull

Hockey Sticks, Ice

Hole Cutter, Golf

Hole Rim, Golf

Horse, Vaulting

Hurdles, Safety

Hurley Goods

Indian Clubs

Jackets—
    Fencing
    Foot Ball

Javelins

Jerseys

Knee Protectors

Lacrosse

Lanes for Sprints

Lawn Bowls

Leg Guards—
    Base Ball
    Cricket
    Foot Ball

Markers, Tennis

Masks—
    Base Ball
    Fencing
    Nose

Masseur, Abdominal

Mattresses

Megaphones

Mitts—
    Base Ball

Handball
  Striking Bag

Moccasins

Nets—
  Cricket
  Golf Driving
  Tennis
  Volley Ball

Numbers, Competitors'

Pads—
  Chamois, Fencing
  Foot Ball
  Sliding, Base Ball

Pants—
  Base Ball
  Basket Ball
  Foot Ball, College
  Foot Ball, Rugby
  Hockey, Ice
  Running

Pennants, College

Plates—
  Base Ball Shoe
  Home
  Marking, Tennis
  Pitchers' Box
  Pitchers' Toe
  Teeing, Golf

Platforms, Striking Bag

Poles—
   Vaulting

Polo, Roller, Goods

Posts—
   Backstop, Tennis
   Lawn Tennis

Protectors—
   Abdomen
   Base Ball Body
   Eye Glass

Push Ball

Quoits

Rackets, Tennis

Rings—
   Exercising
   Swinging

Rowing Machines

Roque

Sacks, for Sack Racing

Score Board, Golf

Score Books

Score Tablets, Base Ball

Shirts—
   Athletic
   Base Ball

Shoes—

Base Ball
Basket Ball
Bowling
Clog
Cross Country
Cricket
Fencing
Foot Ball, Association
Foot Ball, College
Foot Ball, Rugby
Foot Ball, Soccer
Golf
Gymnasium
Jumping
Running
Skating
Squash
Tennis

Shot—
Athletic
Indoor
Massage

Skates—
Ice
Roller

Skis

Sleeve, Pitchers

Snow Shoes

Squash Goods

Straps—
Base Ball
For Three-Legged Race

Skate

Stockings

Striking Bags

Suits—
Basket Ball
Gymnasium
Gymnasium, Ladies'
Running
Soccer
Swimming
Union Foot Ball

Supporters
Ankle
Wrist

Suspensories

Sweaters

Tether Tennis

Tights—
Full
Wrestling
Knee

Toboggans

Trapeze

Trunks—
Bathing
Velvet
Worsted

Umpire Indicator Uniforms

Wands, Calisthenic

Watches, Stop

Water Wings

Weights, 56-lb.

Whitely Exercisers

Wrestling Equipment

Standard Policy

A Standard Quality must be inseparably linked to a Standard Policy.

Without a definite and Standard Mercantile Policy, it is impossible for a manufacturer to long maintain a Standard Quality.

To market his goods through the jobber, a manufacturer must provide a profit for the jobber as well as the retail dealer. To meet these conditions of Dual Profits, the manufacturer is obliged to set a proportionately high list price on his goods to the consumer.

To enable the glib salesman, when booking his orders, to figure out attractive profits to both the jobber and retailer, these high list prices are absolutely essential; but their real purpose will have been served when the manufacturer has secured his order from the jobber, and the jobber has secured his order from the retailer.

However, these deceptive high list prices are not fair to the consumer, who does not, and, in reality, is not ever expected to pay these fancy list prices.

When the season opens for the sale of such goods, with their misleading but alluring high list prices, the retailer begins to realize his responsibilities, and grapples with the situation as best he can, by offering "special discounts," which vary with local trade conditions.

Under this system of merchandising, the profits to both the manufacturer and the jobber are assured; but as there is no stability maintained in the prices to the consumer, the keen competition amongst the local dealers invariably leads to a demoralized cutting of prices by which the profits of the retailer are practically eliminated.

This demoralization always reacts on the manufacturer. The jobber insists on lower, and still lower, prices. The manufacturer, in his turn, meets this demand for the lowering of prices by the only way open to him, viz.: the cheapening and degrading of the quality of his product.

The foregoing conditions became so intolerable that, ten years ago, in 1899, A. G. Spalding & Bros. determined to rectify this demoralization in the Athletic Goods Trade, and inaugurated what has since become known as "The Spalding Policy."

The "Spalding Policy" eliminates the jobber entirely, so far as Spalding Goods are concerned, and the retail dealer secures his supply of Spalding Athletic Goods direct from the manufacturer under a restricted retail price arrangement by which the retail dealer is assured a fair, legitimate and certain profit on all Spalding Athletic Goods, and the consumer is assured a Standard Quality and is protected from imposition.

The "Spalding Policy" is decidedly for the interest and protection of the users of Athletic Goods, and acts in two ways:

First—The user is assured of genuine Official Standard Athletic Goods, and the same fixed prices to everybody.

Second—As manufacturers, we can proceed with confidence in purchasing at the proper time, the very best raw materials required in the manufacture of our various goods, well ahead of their respective seasons, and this enables us to provide the necessary quantity and absolutely maintain the Spalding Standard of Quality.

All retail dealers handling Spalding Athletic Goods are required to supply consumers at our regular printed catalogue prices—neither more nor less—the same prices that similar goods are sold for in our New York, Chicago and other stores.

All Spalding dealers, as well as users of Spalding Athletic Goods, are treated exactly alike, and no special rebates or discriminations are allowed to anyone.

Positively, nobody; not even officers, managers, salesmen or other employes of A. G. Spalding & Bros., or any of their relatives or personal friends, can buy Spalding Athletic Goods at a discount from the regular catalogue prices.

This, briefly, is the "Spalding Policy," which has already been in successful operation for the past ten years, and will be indefinitely continued.

In other words, "The Spalding Policy" is a "square deal" for everybody.

A. G. SPALDING & BROS.

By *A. G. Spalding.*

PRESIDENT.

www.ingramcontent.com/pod-product-compliance
Lightning Source LLC
Chambersburg PA
CBHW020233030726
47497CB00009B/3079